Oh, Bother! SOMEONE'S FIGHTING!

Story by Nikki Grimes

Illustrated by Darrell Baker

A GOLDEN BOOK • NEW YORK

Western Publishing Company, Inc., Racine, Wisconsin 53404

T5.25

One afternoon Eeyore carried a bundle of thistles to the far side of his gloomy place. He set them down, stacked them neatly, sighed, then carried them back to their original spot. Eeyore had done the same thing ten times already. It wasn't a very interesting way to spend an afternoon, but then Eeyore had nothing better to do.

"It sure would be nice if someone came by to visit," thought Eeyore. "No one will, of course. They never do. And why should they?"

Just then Tigger bounced up. "Hello, Eeyore!" said Tigger. "Oh, hello, Tigger," said Eeyore. "This is a surprise! No one ever comes to visit me. Not that I blame them. This is a visit, isn't it?" he asked hopefully.

"Course it is!" said Tigger. "Us Tiggers like doing all that neighbory-type stuff, like visiting friends. I'm not interrupting anything, am I? You weren't doing anything special, were you?"

"Me?" asked Eeyore. "Not really. Just moving this bundle of thistles. Would you like to join me? Moving thistles?"

Tigger looked at the bundle of thistles and shook his head. "Buddy boy," said Tigger. "You need to get out more and do things."

Tigger paced back and forth, thinking. "What you really need," said Tigger, "is to go bouncing. Why, it's the most fun thing you could do. And I ought to know, because bouncing is what Tiggers do best!"

"Well," said Eeyore, "Tiggers may be very good at bouncing, but I'm not. Besides, if I tried bouncing like you, my tail would come off. It always does, you know. And then where would I be?"

Tiger continued pacing back and forth, trying to think of something else Eeyore might go out and do. In the middle of all that pacing, Rabbit came whistling by, carrying a brand-new shovel and spade.

"Good afternoon, Eeyore," said Rabbit.

"Hello," answered Eeyore. "Is it a good afternoon? I doubt it."

"Hiya, Rabbit!" greeted Tigger.

"Out for your afternoon bounce, Tigger?" asked Rabbit.

"Exactly! And I was just telling my buddy here that he should try it—'specially since he needs to get out and do something."

"Then he should try gardening," suggested Rabbit. "It's quite relaxing, you know. I recommend it highly."

Eeyore tried to picture himself in a garden. He imagined holding a spade and digging holes in the earth for planting seeds. But what kind of seeds?

"This garden," asked Eeyore, "would it be a vegetable garden?"

"Why, yes, of course," replied Rabbit. "That's the very best sort of garden there is."

"Never mind," said Eeyore. "I don't like vegetables. Not very much. Not at all, actually. But thanks for the suggestion."

"I don't blame you, buddy boy," said Tigger. "What kind of fun is working in a garden, anyway?"

"Oh, really?" snapped Rabbit, throwing down his shovel and stabbing his spade into the ground. "And what's so great about your silly bouncing? Tell me that!"

"Does anybody want to know what I—" began Eeyore, but he never finished his sentence. Tigger and Rabbit were so busy arguing with each other, they forget that Eeyore was even there.

"What's all the fuss?" asked a very small voice. Eeyore, Rabbit, and Tigger spun around. It was Piglet.

"Let's ask Piglet," said Rabbit, gritting his teeth.

"Ask me what?" Piglet wanted to know.

"Eeyore needs to get out more, and we're trying to find something for him to go out and do. Like *gardening*," stressed Rabbit.

"Or *bouncing*," put in Tigger.

"Which thing should Eeyore go out and do?" asked Rabbit.

"That's easy!" answered Piglet. "When Pooh and I have nothing special planned, we go on a long explore. That's always fun!"

"Not an explore!" said Tigger emphatically. "He'll get lost!"

"Besides," added Rabbit, "it's too late in the day to begin a long explore. It would be dark before Eeyore found his way home."

"Exactly," agreed Tigger. "Bouncing is a much better idea!"

"No! Gardening!" yelled Rabbit.

"Bouncing!" Tigger yelled right back.

Piglet sighed. "I g-guess my idea wasn't so good after all," he muttered.

Eeyore glumly returned to his bundle of thistles. It saddened him to see his friends fighting—especially over him. "I wish I knew how to make everyone happy," thought Eeyore.

Just then Winnie the Pooh arrived. "A party!" said Pooh, clapping his hands. "What fun! Am I invited?"

"It's not a p-party, Pooh," said Piglet. "It's more like a f-fight.

"Eeyore needs to get out more, and Tigger thinks he should go out bouncing. Rabbit thinks he should start a vegetable garden, and I told Eeyore he should go on a long explore. It's no use, Pooh," said Piglet, sighing. "We just can't agree."

"Oh, my," said Pooh. "That doesn't sound like much fun at all. I wonder what Christopher Robin would suggest."

Unfortunately, Christopher Robin was not around to suggest anything, so Rabbit, Tigger, and Piglet went right on arguing while Eeyore moved his bundle of thistles for the millionth time.

"All this fighting sure does make me hungry," said Pooh. "I've got a rumbly in my tumbly. Eeyore? I don't suppose you'd have a pot of honey hidden somewhere, would you? Otherwise, I think I'll just have to go home and see if I can find a little something in my cupboard."

"That's it!" cried Piglet excitedly. "A picnic! Why don't we all go on a picnic, Eeyore? That would be a great something to get out and do, wouldn't it?"

"Why, Piglet," said Pooh. "What a splendid idea!"

"Yeah!" agreed Tigger. "I could bounce all the way there."

"And I could bring fresh vegetables from my garden!" said Rabbit.

"And I could run home and get a pot of honey for dessert!" added Pooh.

"Well, Eeyore," said Piglet. "What do you think?"

"It isn't a terrible idea," admitted Eeyore. "At least it's better than all this fighting."

Later, Eeyore and his friends met for their picnic. Everyone seemed happy—except Piglet. He still wanted to go on a long explore, but Eeyore knew that soon it would be too dark.

"You know," Eeyore said to everyone. "I think we should all go on a short explore when the picnic's over. Piglet, would you and Pooh lead us? That way we won't get lost."

"Sure!" said Piglet, grinning.

When Eeyore looked around his circle of smiling friends, he couldn't help but smile, too—in spite of himself!